This Walker Book
Belongs to:

. . . .

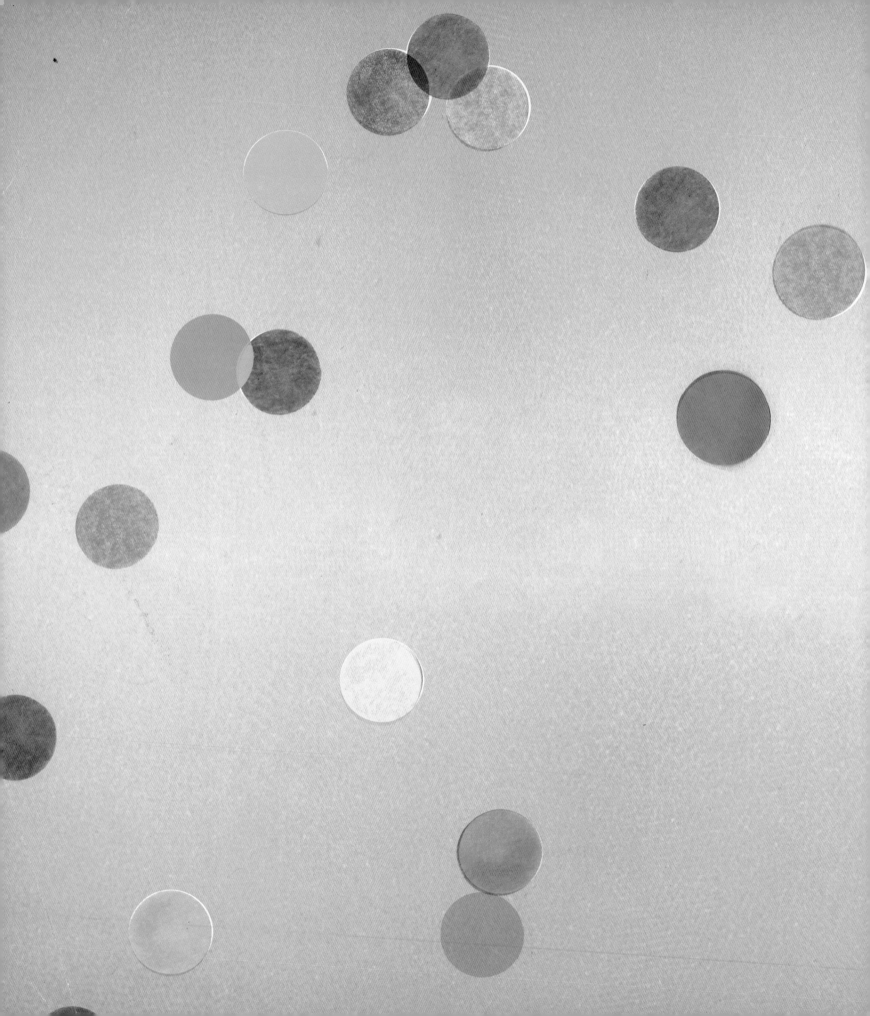

First published 2015 by Walker Books Ltd
87 Vauxhall Walk, London SE11 5HJ

This edition published 2016

2 4 6 8 10 9 7 5 3 1

Text © 2015 Joyce Dunbar
Illustrations © 2015 Polly Dunbar

The right of Joyce Dunbar and Polly Dunbar
to be identified as author and illustrator
respectively of this work has been asserted
by them in accordance with the Copyright,
Designs and Patents Act 1988

This book has been typeset in
PF Playskool Pro

Printed in China

British Library Cataloguing
in Publication Data:
a catalogue record for this book is
available from the British Library

ISBN 978-1-4063-6580-1

www.walker.co.uk

WALKER BOOKS
AND SUBSIDIARIES

LONDON · BOSTON · SYDNEY · AUCKLAND

For Mabel
and Pearl

written by Joyce Dunbar

Pat-a-Cake
BABY

illustrated by Polly Dunbar

I'm a cookie baby
a pat-a-cake baby
I want to bake
a very special cake
while everyone is sleeping, but...

THE KITCHEN'S WIDE AWAKE.

IT'S WAKING TIME!

So I'm rolling out the bowl
and my spoon is at the ready

for Candy Baby's helping
and Jelly Baby's jumping
and Allsorts Baby's

laughing

'cos they're

oops-a-daisy

bumping.

IT'S BAKING TIME!

With a mutter mutter mutter
pitter patter comes the butter
oh so yellow shiny yellow

And here's the sugar, ditzy sugar,
oh so **GLITZY** oh so **GLOSSY**
and we're frisking while we're whisking 'til it's

flitter flotter

And the eggs say, "Let's get cracking!"

They're yolky and they're jokey

and they're **diving** and they're **smacking**

and they slither and they slide.

Here's some milk all in a sulk
what's it for for for?
We sip it slop it tip it to make it

Now the flour's in a shower
we are sieving shaking sieving
and we're snowy yes we're showy
and it's

all so very blowy.

It's so sweet, oh just so sweet
our spiffy special cake
for a magic midnight treat.

IT'S HULLA-

IT'S

BALLOONY-MOON-TIME!

So we've put it in the tin
and the tin into the oven
and we smell it while we cook it

steaming   smelling   sniffing.

We're scraping out the bowl
with an icky flicky licky
and oops we lick each other
and all of us are sticky.

And can you see our cake
RISING RISING RISING
and I've got a funny feeling
it will rise up to the

squiggle

the cake

balls and jelly diamonds

we
scatter
scatter
hundreds
and
sprinkle

spronkle
thousands.

And our cake is very gooey
chewy yimmy yummy
and we think we're very clever
did you ever ever ever
see a cake that's

Here's a slice for you

and a slice for me

AND LOOK WHO'S JUST TURNED UP FOR TEA!

TIME!

Joyce Dunbar has had several books published by Walker Books including *Baby Bird, Gander's Pond, Panda's New Toy, The Secret Friend, Tutti Frutti, The Monster Who Ate Darkness* and *Shoe Baby*, illustrated by her daughter Polly. *Pat-a-Cake Baby,* Joyce's second picture book collaboration with her daughter, was the winner of the Mal Peet Children's Award at the East Anglian Book Awards. Joyce lives in Norwich.

Find Joyce online at www.joycedunbar.com

Polly Dunbar is the author-illustrator of *Arthur's Dream Boat* and the best-selling picture book *Penguin,* winner of numerous awards including the Book Trust Early Years Award and the Red House Children's Book of the Year Award. She is also the illustrator of *My Dad's a Birdman,* by David Almond, and *Shoe Baby,* written by her mother, Joyce Dunbar. Her collection of titles beginning with *Hello Tilly* were made into an animation series, *Tilly and Friends,* as seen on CBeebies. She is the co-founder of Long Nose Puppets, a children's theatre company who have adapted *Pat-a-Cake Baby* for their tenth anniversary show. Polly lives in Brighton, Sussex.

Find Polly online at www.pollydunbar.com, and on Twitter as @PollyDunbar
Find out more about Long Nose Puppets' upcoming shows at www.longnosepuppets.com

Also by Joyce and Polly Dunbar:

978-1-4063-0161-8

Available from all good booksellers

www.walker.co.uk